GRIT IN JUAREZ

GRIT IN JUAREZ

BEYOND THE WALL

MARION SURLES

Love and Literacy

Published by Love and Literacy

ISBN 978-0-578-44492-5

Typesetting services by BOOKOW.COM

For Betzi

Preface

Ciudad Juarez, Mexico
2018

The city of Ciudad Juarez, Mexico, lies just across the Rio Grande, a shallow ditch of a river, from the modern city of El Paso, Texas. Juarez has modern factories, mostly US companies, lining the border called maquiladoras, or maquilas for short. They attract desperate people to the city to work and find places to live. These families have built little huts of pallets, cardboard, and tarps hoping they can make enough money someday to build something better. This story takes place in one of those neighborhoods.

ACKNOWLEDGMENTS

To Maricela and Pablo who opened their home and became family. To Jay Nutt who inspired me to write and provided space for escuelita, humor, and so much more. To the niños of Suleiman, Ciudad Juarez, may reading open doors for your dreams. To the many supporters of Love and Literacy who have sent me books and donations. To my DeLeon UMC family and friends and family who have prayed for me. TO MY LONG-SUFFERING HUSBAND WHO SUPPORTS ALL MY ADVENTURES. Thank you, Lord, for trusting me with this opportunity.

Whoever welcomes one of these children in my name welcomes me.
Mark 9:37

Chapter 1

CRISTAL

CRISTAL stretched and tensed under the pile of dirty clothes, trying to stay warm. Halfway between awake and asleep, she tried to continue her dream about a warm bed. She usually had nightmares of someone chasing her. This dream was a nice change, but she couldn't go back to sleep. Her nose smelled the damp pee smell that told her Fina wet her pants in the night. She didn't smell any smoke from the fire so she knew their mamá Rubí hadn't come home again last night. She also needed to go to the bathroom but didn't want to venture outside until the sun came up a little. "The sun is a poor man's blanket" she had heard someone say. She knew all about that. She didn't remember ever having her own blanket.

The door slammed and Cristal's older brother Ivan came in from his run to the outside toilet. It was really just a scary hole in the ground with raggedy curtains around it. Some of their neighbors had fiberglass outhouses with a real seat. A government office gave them out for free, but her mamá never signed them up for one. Just like she never signed them up for school.

Cristal finally made herself get up. She wrapped herself in two dirty sweaters and went to the outhouse. She grabbed a bucket of water from the big barrel in front of their house. At least the water truck had stopped by yesterday when she was there so they could get their one free fill-up for the week. Cristal grabbed some cardboard scraps and some pieces of a broken pallet and went inside to start the fire in the little stove-pipe heater. She heated some water and made them some instant coffee with sugar containing a few ants. There were three tortillas left that she heated up on the *comal*. She made little Fina take off the wet pants, wipe off with a little of the warm water, and put on some other pants. Everything was dirty. Mamá never washed clothes. She just threw the clothes in a pile and waited for some more missionary donations.

The wind blew through the cloth hanging over the only window blowing dirt and dust all through the house. Even so, they were lucky now that they had a cinderblock house. It was the same size as their pallet house they had in this same spot but was a little more dependable. Cristal remembered the pallet house. Last winter it snowed. She had never been so cold. Pallets and cardboard dragged from the garbage heap formed the walls. The roof was made of tarps. Someone brought tarps across the border to donate to the needy families in their neighborhood. They had gotten a big strong tarp with some kind of advertising on it. It didn't leak, but it still wasn't warm.

The scary part was the electricity. They were far away from the closest electric pole. Their papá was around some back then. He ran a cable over 100 meters from the high-tension power pole to their house. They hung a single lightbulb inside the hut. They had a microwave then too that they used some if the neighbor wasn't using too much electricity at the same time. But then came the terrible dust storm last fall followed by a terrible rainstorm. Everything was covered in mud. And in the middle of the night their little house collapsed. They had run screaming to a neighbor's house who took them in. But, only for that one night. The neighbor had six children of her own.

That was when Papá left. A few men had helped them prop up the pallets again, but the electricity was too dangerous even for them. No one would help with that. Then Mamá got the news that a group would be building them a block house. Before the group arrived to build it in January, the snow had fallen. For just a few minutes the neighborhood was clean, white, and bright, but so very, very cold. Cristal often wondered what it would be like to have a bath, clean clothes, and a clean house, to be clean like the snow.

She scratched her head vigorously as she watched two lice crawling in her sister's head. Cristal knew she must have lice too. But what could she do? Nobody really cared about them.

Ivan ran out the door without a goodbye. Cristal grabbed Fina's hand and put a few more layers of clothes on both of them. They headed to the dump, hoping to find enough scrap metal to sell for some more tortillas. They were kids, just 10, 8, and 6, but they were old beyond their years in survival.

Chapter 2

DANIEL

A few streets over, Daniel snuggled back under his heavy blankets and pushed his little brother Memo's foot as he did. Memo snarled but snuggled down too at the other end of the bed. They shared a twin bed now, one sleeping with his head one way and the other the other way. Most of the time it was a good fix. But sometimes Memo kicked and screamed and pulled off all the covers. Daniel listened for his mamá Araceli to get up and turn the electric heater back on. His papá would be home soon from his night shift at the *maquila*. Mamá would fix them a big breakfast of eggs and chorizo, frijoles, tortillas, and chocolate milk. Then he would do his *tarea* for school and Papá would go to the back room to sleep. Daniel didn't have school until 1:00 so he could stay in the bed a little longer.

Daniel barely remembered the pallet house with the tarp roof. He did remember having the wood stove for heat. It kept the house pretty warm, but the thought of it scared him to death. He could still see his baby brother Memo wrapped in a blanket and slowly turning purple. His mamá was screaming for his papá to do something. They grabbed Memo and Daniel and ran to the nearest bus stop to get to the emergency clinic. Daniel was so cold and scared. He hadn't really understood what was happening, but soon the runs to the clinic became routine to Daniel. But, the fear that accompanied him never would. They were also kids, 8 and 4, but they were learning that life was not always safe and certain.

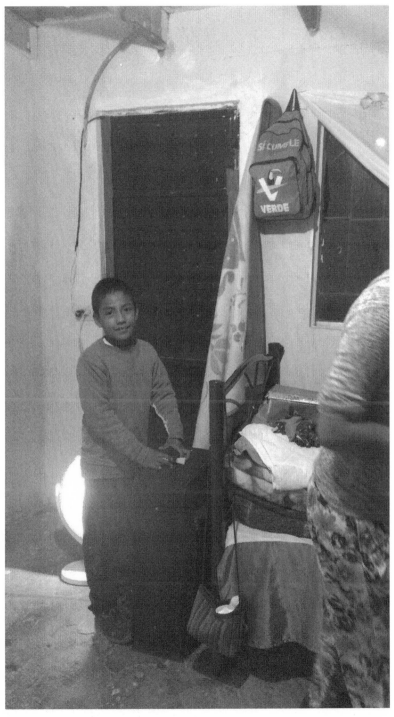

Chapter 3

THE PASTORS

THE little block church had a flapping tarp roof covering two small rooms. Pastora Pati and her husband Pastor Miguel were unloading sound equipment at *Iglesia Torre de Fe*, Tower of Faith Church. They also had a keyboard, an electric guitar, a projector, a Bible, and printed programs for the service that day. Other churches in the neighborhood had already cranked up the volume of their sound equipment shouting invitations to anyone who could hear. Their church joined the noise.

Pastora Pati and a couple of young people led blaring praise music for 45 minutes. Then Pastor Miguel shouted his message to the few in the congregation for over an hour. He felt he needed to make sure they got a good enough dose of scripture, fear, and need for repentance to last them a week. Then they were good to go. Other churches followed suit, *Templo de Alabanza, La Iglesia de los Milagros, La Capilla de Dolores*, plus many Catholic masses. There were groups of Jehovah's Witness and Latter Day Saints on Saturday, too. But Monday through Friday, nothing seemed to change in the community. The worship services didn't seem to have any effect. Life was hard, and the children suffered.

Chapter 4

CRISTAL

CRISTAL and Fina walked all over the dump site watching for anything that could be a good find. Aluminum cans were usually picked up quick and had to be saved in a safe place until there were enough to sell. Scrap metal was a quicker turnover. Each girl carried a plastic bag they found along the way, one from the Bodega, one from S-Mart. Fina always looked for pretty magazine pages she wanted to save. Cristal let her as long as she carried her part of anything else they found. Maybe the pictures were her hopes and dreams.

The sisters also kept an eye out for snakes, scorpions, and bullies. For now, they at least both had shoes that pretty much fit. The heat from the ground was beginning to burn her feet through her worn out *chanclas*. The desert climate was severe, so cold at night, but so hot in the day.

An old pick-up eased along the worn gravel road through the dump dodging potholes. Cristal and Fina hid behind an old mattress. The truck stopped and two men got out to unload a big pile of stuff.

"Thank you," whispered Cristal to no one in particular. She just knew that the men dumping their things right where she and her sister were hiding was a big advantage. They would have first dibs. The men pulled away, and the girls began to dig in the pile. Cristal found three pieces of metal pipe, an old car tag, and a few pieces of bent tin. Fina found an almost used up watercolor set and a rusty pair of children's scissors. Cristal let her keep them if she would carry the tag and the tin.

They started the long walk back to the neighborhood, stopping at a hole to take care of their business, using newspaper scraps to clean up. That was something their mama had taught them.

They stopped at Don Diego's house and sold the scrap. The other kids called them *kileras*, a teasing nickname because they made money by the kilo.

They stopped at the little store and bought a stack of tortillas and a 2-liter Coke, having to use some of their money for the deposit on the bottle. The other children Cristal's age had already walked to school. The sun overhead was scorching now as the stray dogs found shade for the afternoon. Cristal and Fina made it home just as their mamá was waking up.

"Bring me a Coke," she hollered at them. Cristal quickly poured her mamá some Coke in a dirty cup. "What else you got?"

"Just tortillas," said Cristal.

"I got a paint set!" said Fina happily as she got out her prizes from the dump. Mamá didn't make any comment.

"Where's your brother?" Mamá asked. "Why hasn't he fixed that door yet?"

Cristal didn't want to be responsible for him too. She already had to take Fina with her everywhere she went. Ivan was older than she was. He could answer for himself. But she didn't dare say her thoughts out loud. "He'll be home soon" was all she said.

Mamá looked through the pile of clothes and found something cleaner than what she had on. She changed right in front of them. That still embarrassed Cristal. She stirred up the stove again and heated some more tortillas. Mamá had brought home a can of beans, so Cristal opened it and heated enough for all three of them, probably their only meal for the day.

The little television was blaring a *novela* so there was little need for conversation. Soon they heard the little neighbor Aida from next door calling her dog, so Cristal and Fina slipped outside again.

Aida was in kindergarten and went to school from 8:00-12:30. She always played with them in the afternoon until the older kids came home. Aida was smart. Her mamá read books to her and told her stories. Aida could write her name and the numbers 1-10. She liked to play school, and Cristal loved it. She absorbed everything they played. Aida was always the teacher. Cristal understood numbers and could count and add and subtract in her head. She was learning to form the letters of Aida's name and anything else that Aida wanted to "teach". Aida's mamá sometimes came out and showed her how to write her name too. Cristal just knew she could be a good student if she had the chance. She tried to help Fina too. Maybe next year Fina could go to school even if Cristal couldn't. But she didn't know how they would ever get the money for the registration, much less the uniform.

The girls drew off the hopscotch pattern in the dirt. No grass grew anywhere so the pattern pretty much blew away every day. They played for a long time, Fina finally remembering her numbers as she jumped. Then they played house and made some mud tortillas. Cristal wished it was real food. Her stomach growled.

Chapter 5

DANIEL

DANIEL came out of his classroom door. "See you tomorrow, Maestra," he said. His teacher smiled and waved at his mamá. Memo was running around with the other little brothers and sisters whose mamás were waiting in the pick-up line. A few stray dogs always joined in the fun and somehow found their families as the crowd surged out the gate.

Some families stopped for *chucherías,* a candied apple or a bag of *chicharrones con salsa.* But Daniel and Memo knew not to ask. Mamá had to save every peso to pay all the bills. Besides Mamá always had a good supper ready when Daniel got home from school. Papá would have already eaten and gone to his night shift from 6-6. But most mornings he would play soccer with the boys for a little while before he went to bed.

"Any homework, Daniel?" his mamá asked.

"Just one page of math. I finished the vocabulary words at school." Daniel was a good reader. He was chosen to compete in a reading competition next month at his school. Numbers were harder for him. That was funny to him because his papá couldn't read but could do numbers. His papá was pretty impatient with him when he made mistakes in math. Daniel kicked a plastic bottle toward Memo, and Memo kicked it farther down the road. They continued on taking turns, pretending the bottle was a soccer ball, gradually collecting more players from the neighborhood as they walked.

"Come wash your hands and eat, Daniel," his mamá said as they got to their yard. Daniel hung up his backpack and took out the snack container his mamá packed him every day. He was the only one who brought pieces of fruit or slices of cucumber with chile as a snack. Most kids either brought nothing or had a few pesos to buy *Sabritas* or *Gansitos* at the gate. Daniel washed his hands and sat down to eat. Mamá had cooked rice, beans, and *chile colorado*. He used the tortillas as his spoon. Each strip was a new spoon. He remembered his papá had bragged that even the poorest Mexican was like a king, eating each bite with a different spoon.

When Daniel finished, he and Memo went outside to play with their cars and trucks in the dirt. They built ramps and racetracks and pretended to be El Chavo and friends. Memo had a runny nose and wiped it with a dirty shirtsleeve. Mamá called them in as it got dark, and Daniel turned on the TV. A soccer match of the team Santos was on. They watched and yelled "Goooooooal" with the announcer each time their team scored. Memo coughed at the end of each yell. Mamá gave him a spoonful of medicine and a spoonful of honey. She always looked worried whenever Memo sniffed or coughed. Sometimes Daniel felt jealous that Memo got so much attention. Then he felt bad that he felt that way, but he couldn't help it.

Daniel got one of his books from his backpack and began to read. He really liked animal stories. Maybe one day he would be an animal doctor.

"Stop it, Memo," Daniel said in a loud voice. Memo was always pestering him when he tried to read.

"Read to him, Daniel," said his mamá. "He needs to learn to listen to the teacher. He could start school next year in pre-K."

Daniel read some out loud, but Memo quickly began to pester with his feet, trying to put one foot up into Daniel's face. "Stop it," Daniel shouted again. This time Mamá grabbed Memo and took him to read to him alone. He missed his mamá reading to him too. He liked to read, but he liked for her to read chapter books to him too. Sometimes Memo seemed to get all the good stuff. It didn't seem fair.

Chapter 6

CRISTAL

Aida's mamá called her in to eat. Cristal and Fina sadly began walking around the neighborhood. A mean boy named Toño called out to them, "Where's your mamá, Gorditas?"

They tried to ignore him. He was always causing trouble. They turned down another street and tried to think of something to do or somewhere to eat. Sometimes there was a *comedor* that let them eat for free, but it was closed today. They kept walking and saw the daughter of the store keeper playing outside. Aurora was always laughing and having fun. Being three silly girls helped them to forget that they were hungry for a little while. But soon Aurora had to go in too, so they continued on.

The wind was blowing harder and the dust caught in their eyes. Fina wanted to cry but knew that crying would just make it worse. They passed a little church where they could hear singing. A loud microphone carried the man's voice, yelling louder and louder that the people needed Jesus as their savior. Cristal wished that that Jesus would come save them. They walked circles around the neighborhood until dark, but no one offered them anything. They went home and ate a cold tortilla. As usual, Mamá had already gone out, and they were hungry and alone. They soon fell asleep on a pile of dirty clothes like two abandoned puppies.

Chapter 7

DANIEL

DANIEL finished his breakfast and got out his math homework. He wanted to finish quickly so his papá would play soccer with him before he went to sleep. But Memo kept trying to mark on his paper. "Stop it, Memo," he shouted at his brother. Papá finished his last bite and took Memo outside to work on the old car.

Memo always got to do fun stuff. It wasn't fair. He finished the paper quickly and stuffed it in his backpack, turning to run outside with Memo and Papá. But Mamá grabbed his shoulder and said, "Let me check that first." His shoulders sagged as he waited for what he knew would cost him more time inside.

Chapter 8

CRISTAL AND DANIEL

CRISTAL and Fina were on their third round of the neighborhood when they saw Daniel and Memo come out to play soccer. The girls watched as the boys played with their papá. Cristal wondered what that was like. She had never played with either one of her parents. She was about to move on when Daniel's mamá came out. Cristal had seen her before. She sometimes visited their neighbor. They smiled at each other, but Cristal kept walking. Araceli waved at her to come over calling, "Don't you girls want a burrito this morning?"

Cristal hesitated, but Fina ran as she shouted, "Yes, we do".

Cristal came up behind Fina and said quietly, "*Sí, Señora.*"

Araceli went inside and soon came back out with two cheese and bean burritos and two juice boxes. The girls said thank you and began to eat the burritos as fast as they could. They were so hungry. While they ate, Araceli asked them a few questions.

"Where's your mamá working now?"

"I don't know," mumbled Cristal.

"Has your mamá gotten you enrolled for school yet?"

"Don't know," said Cristal.

"Do you have something to eat for later?"

"I don't know," said Cristal a little embarrassed.

Araceli went back inside. She brought a small bag with two apples and two small yogurts. She also had some kind of workbook.

"Cristal, do you want to practice your letters here?" She showed her a dry-erase marker that she could wipe off with her fingers and practice over and over. "The group building houses left this for Daniel, but he already knows his letters and Memo is too little yet. You can have it and use it until the marker runs out."

"Thank you, Señora," said Cristal and then more softly, "but I don't know what they are. I can copy them, but I don't know what they do."

"I can help with that," Araceli said. "You can come by during the week about one o'clock, and we can work together. Daniel will be gone to school, and my husband will be asleep. Maybe Memo too. But not today because it's Friday, and my husband is home."

Cristal was thrilled but also a little worried. She never knew what day it was. One hungry day ran into another. She was glad to know it was Friday because she knew that tomorrow there was a *comedor* open on Saturdays. She could eat a real meal. Just then a soccer ball hit the side of her head.

"Daniel!" Araceli shouted. Daniel ran up and grabbed the ball mumbling, "I'm sorry," but not making eye contact.

"Are you okay?" Araceli asked.

"Yes, Señora," said Cristal, "We need to go now, gotta look for more scrap. Thank you for the burrito and this." She held up the bag. "We will be back on Monday!" She almost skipped to the dump, dragging Fina behind her. They passed another church with a lot of letters painted on the wall, but Cristal couldn't read them. One day she would! She looked down at the bag. "Thank you," she said to no one in particular.

Daniel, Memo, and Papá continued to play soccer after the girls walked away. The boys loved getting the ball past Papá and shouting "goooooooal" together. They were loving the extra time to play with Papá, but it always ended too soon.

"Time to get ready for school, Daniel." Memo got to keep playing outside with his cars. Papá did help Daniel bathe and dress in his school uniform. He also shined his shoes and brushed his hair, slicking it to the side the way he liked it. Mamá fixed his snack box and a water bottle for his backpack. Then it was time to go. Papá lay down to catch up on the sleep he lost during the night shift.

Mamá walked Daniel to school with Memo in tow sniffing and wiping his dirty nose on his shirtsleeve. Daniel walked beside them leaning back from the weight of his backpack. The wind picked up more dust and dirt from the grassless yards. Daniel's clean white uniform shirt had a beige color to it now. Memo coughed, and Mamá got that worried look on her face that always scared Daniel.

"I'm gonna let you walk the rest of the way by yourself. Here comes Richi and Dulce. I need to get Memo out of this wind." Mamá scooped up Memo and headed back home. Daniel joined his friends and their mamás and continued on to school kicking a rock along the way, trying to ignore that jealous feeling he was having again. *Memo is Mamá's favorite. Nobody really cares about me, just Memo.*

Chapter 9

CRISTAL

CRISTAL and Fina found enough scrap metal to buy a tray of eggs. When they got home, Mamá was there frantically hauling out big piles of dirty clothes and garbage.

"Where have you two been?" she screamed. "Get in here and start cleaning. DIF will be here any minute."

Cristal grabbed a ratty broom as Ivan came in with a bucket of water. Together they scrubbed the concrete floor as best they could and tried to make the kitchen look like they actually used it for cooking and eating. Cristal hated when DIF came by. DIF workers were supposed to protect children. But Mamá always told them the sweetest stories of their perfect lives, how Papá would be back soon from his job, and they were all going to the Soriana to get groceries. How the kids were on a waiting list for a school in the next neighborhood because there wasn't any more space in the school in this neighborhood. How she had just gotten back from a job interview at a maquiladora and hoped to start on the opposite shift from their papá so that the kids would never be home alone. How grandparents were helping them out with food. So many lies so easily told. It made Cristal's stomach hurt, but she kept her mouth shut. They had been picked up by DIF once, and she never wanted to have that happen again.

Finally, the house was fairly clean with a few clothes stacked for each child in a cabinet. Cristal stirred up a fire in the little stove and heated the *comal*. She scrambled some eggs and heated the remaining tortillas. They were all sitting together eating when the DIF car pulled up. They looked like the perfect family having a meal together. Mamá answered the usual questions as the social worker glanced quickly around the one-room block house. Satisfied or maybe just checking off that she had visited, the lady left. And just as quickly, so did Mamá.

Chapter 10

DANIEL

DANIEL and Memo woke up early even though it was Saturday. They had all day to play and no responsibilities. They tussled in the bed and watched Pokemon cartoons until Mamá and Papá decided to get up. They folded their blankets the way Papá liked them and went outside to play.

Daniel hoped that maybe he could go with Papá to the *segundas* to sell stuff. He should have taken his time with the math sheets this week. He always made silly mistakes when he hurried. Then Papá would say, "How can you help me at the *segundas* if you can't make change? I don't need a helper that I always have to be checking behind. You're gonna give away all our hard-earned money." That really made Daniel think. He would work harder on his math facts and take his time on word problems.

But for now, Daniel played some more with Memo alternating riding his scooter and racing the matchbox cars down the little track they made in the dirt. The wind blew the dust around, and Memo wiped his nose on his sleeve and coughed a little.

"Stop it, Memo!" Daniel growled at his little brother. "Don't go getting sick today and ruining our weekend!" They kept playing in the dirt and out in the street with the scooter until Mamá called them to come eat.

Mamá immediately gave Memo more medicine and talked about maybe needing to give him a breathing treatment. The boys ate quietly, and Mamá and Papá talked about what all to sell at the *segundas*. Daniel loved to go sell because he always got to buy some new toy. One time his papá let him buy a broken remote-control car. Papá fixed it quickly, and they enjoyed it for a long time. He hoped Papá would let him go today.

Just then they heard one of the neighbor boys hollering Daniel's name. Daniel ran to open the door and he heard him say, "Daniel, someone just ran off with your scooter!"

Daniel ran outside followed by his papá who was shouting the question he didn't want to answer.

"Where did you leave it, Daniel? I told you to bring it in every time! Why won't you listen? You don't care about anything I buy you. I work all week for you to just leave things out in the street. Get in the house. You can stay home with your mamá and mop floors."

Daniel burst into tears and hid his face, running for the door. He watched out of the corner of his eye as Papá loaded up the things to sell into the car, and then Daniel sobbed even louder as he watched Memo load up with Papá and leave for the day. Nobody cared about him. Memo was their favorite.

Chapter 11

CRISTAL

SATURDAY was a good day for Cristal and Fina. They ate the yogurt from Araceli for breakfast and hid the apples for later, hoping Ivan wouldn't find them. Then they played next door with Aida. Her mamá came out for a while and helped Cristal with her new workbook, telling her the names and sounds of each letter as Cristal formed them. But then Aida's family had to go to the Soriana for their groceries for the week. So, Cristal and Fina went down to the *comedor* to eat. Saturday was one of the few days they sure of a meal.

Pastora Pati was very nice and fixed them a plate. She began to tell them a story about someone named Jesus who took some fish and bread and fed 5,000 people. Cristal loved that story. After answering a few questions about the story, the children colored a picture of the man Jesus handing out the food.

"I wish I had been there," Cristal said.

The pastora smiled and hugged her. Cristal tensed up. It felt good, but nobody ever hugged her. She didn't know what to do. The pastora gave them a bag with two bananas and a box of milk. She told them to come to church the next day and hear more about this Jesus. "*Sí Señora, gracias,*" Cristal responded. Fina never really talked, but she smiled at the pastora and let her hug her tight. Then with full stomachs and happy hearts, the girls walked on through the neighborhood.

There was more activity today as people were getting off work early and relaxing in front of their homes. Some soccer games picked up in the streets, and girls grouped up to watch the young men. Cristal didn't know why the girls never played soccer. She would like to play. But she didn't want to be a part of the crowd. The smell of beer was getting stronger as the sun dropped. Cristal knew that smell only brought problems.

Cristal and Fina stayed on the side streets. But suddenly Toño stepped out from behind a building.

"Hey, Gorditas!" he said as he came too close.

"Leave us alone, Toño!" Cristal shouted as Fina began to whimper. But Toño just moved in closer, pushing her against a wall. "Don't, Toño! Stop!"

Chapter 12

DANIEL

DANIEL went inside to face his mamá.

"Daniel, how many times have we told you not to leave the scooter outside? Did you see who took it?"

"No, Mamá," sobbed Daniel, "but why did Memo get to go to the *segundas?*"

"You are a big boy now, Daniel. We expect a lot from you, just as God expects a lot from us. Remember the verse Pastora Pati talked about at the *comedor* just last week?" said Mamá. "To whom much is given, much is required. We have a nice house, Papá has a steady job, Memo has been healthy, we have enough to eat, but we have to take care of those things. A rich man is not rich because of what he has, but because of what he takes care of. God asks us to be responsible for what He gives us. Now help me clean the house. Papá wants you to mop, to knock down the dust that makes Memo cough."

Daniel obeyed but with little enthusiasm. *Why did Mamá have to always bring God into everything? He knew that Bible verse and many more. He was good at memorizing. But what did that have to do with his scooter. Scooters weren't in the Bible. And how about "thou shalt not steal"? That was in the Bible too. Life wasn't fair.*

He worked until almost dark when Mamá finally gave him some pesos to go get a big Coke for Papá. He couldn't wait to get out of the house. All he was good for was running their errands and doing chores. He was tired of it. Maybe he wouldn't go home tonight and see if they even missed him.

He decided to take a long detour to the store. He might even find his scooter while he was out walking.

Daniel avoided the big street soccer game and the park. He didn't feel like talking to anybody. He found a can to kick down the road. He passed the yard where they made cement blocks. Papá said they were not made well and would crumble soon. He said that the people there were not being honest, that it was the same thing as lying.

He passed the house where the man did refrigerator repair in his front yard. There were maybe 15 refrigerators standing there. Nobody could play soccer at that house. It was getting dark, and a big rat ran across the street right in front of him. He tried not to squeal. He saw it run under the edge of the house and squeeze inside. *Disgusting!* He had only seen one tiny mouse in his block house, never a rat.

Daniel turned the corner and heard someone screaming, "Don't, Toño! Stop!"

Daniel hollered "Stop!" before he even thought about it. Toño had that girl Cristal from this morning penned against a wall, laughing at her while Fina sobbed beside her. Daniel pulled him back.

"Look at the little savior," laughed Toño making fun of Daniel. He backed away as if to go, and Daniel slowly let out his breath. But not before Toño made a quick move and punched him in the eye, then walked away laughing, saying, "Little punk" as he strolled off.

Cristal grabbed Fina and whispered thank you. Daniel wanted to cry. His eye hurt. But at least he didn't get a bloody nose.

"Are you ok?" Cristal asked.

"I'm fine," Daniel said. "Just hiding out from my family."

Cristal couldn't imagine why Daniel would say that. His mamá had been so sweet to her and Fina, not just today but many times.

"Why are you hiding? You have such sweet parents," Cristal said.

But before Daniel could answer, a car whizzed up beside them. Daniel's papá was driving.

"Get in, Daniel, now," Papá shouted. "Why are you way over here? You were just supposed to go to the store."

Daniel got in, saw the look on Mamá's face, and heard the ragged sound of Memo's breathing. Daniel got a sick pain in his stomach. Here we go again, he thought, as Papá sped off through the neighborhood, racing to the hospital.

Chapter 13

CRISTAL

SUNDAY morning Cristal and Fina slipped out of the house without waking mamá. Ivan was still asleep too, but Mamá was usually a grouch after Saturday nights. They took their bananas, apples, and box of milk with them. They ate the bananas as they walked, keeping an eye open for Toño. But no one was out much this early on a Sunday. They went down to their secret shady spot at the dump and opened the box of milk, taking turns drinking straight from the little opening. It was a real treat. They hardly ever had milk.

They began to walk through the dump looking for any new piles of junk. They found what looked like a child's car, bent and rusty. Together they dragged it out of the dump and down the street to Don Diego's house. They got a lot of pesos for that piece, and Cristal stuffed them all deep in her pocket. Then, she remembered Toño from last night and gave half the pesos to Fina to stuff in her pocket.

"Don't lose them!" she warned. "Don't even take them out of your pocket for any reason. Nobody needs to know you have them, not even Ivan, and especially not Mamá."

Fina looked like she wanted to cry so Cristal said, "Let's get us each a *chicle*," and Fina was happy again with the promise of gum.

While they were buying *chicle* at the *tiendita*, they heard the music from the church near the *comedor* start up. Soon several women and children began to show up, but very few men. No sign of Toño either. Cristal didn't really want to go. She liked the pastora, but all that yelling on the microphone that she could hear for blocks was a little scary. All that hollering about blood! Instead, she and Fina found a small tree to sit under and listen. The music lasted a long time with lots of *"Gloria a Dios"* shouted between each song. They liked this music, so different from the *reggaetón* blaring from cars during the week.

Finally, the music stopped, and Cristal knew that the shouting on the microphone was about to begin. She wasn't staying for that. She and Fina got up to leave just as a line of children filed out of the church being led by Pastora Pati. She saw the girls and waved them over. "Come to Sunday school with us at the *comedor*," she called. Cristal and Fina followed, recognizing a few kids from the neighborhood including Aida from next door and Aurora from the store. No sign of Daniel or his little brother, and of course, no Toño.

They all sat on the floor of the *comedor* as the pastora told them another story about Jesus. Jesus was a very popular man. People were always crowding around him, wanting to touch him and talk to him. One day a bunch of mamás came with all their kids, trying to see him. Jesus' friends started running them off. But Jesus told them to stop. He wanted to sit each child on his lap and talk to each one. He said that heaven is like little children.

The pastora kept talking about heaven and explaining their craft project, but Cristal was still trying to figure out what that meant. How was heaven like little kids? Would kids be in charge? What if Toño was in charge? He was still a kid. This Jesus seemed nice to kids, but it was so confusing.

Cristal and Fina colored the picture of Jesus and the children. They were supposed to color the child in his lap to look like themselves. Cristal didn't even have a mirror at home. How was she supposed to know how to color herself? She looked at Fina's paper and decided that she could color hers for her. She made long, black hair with white specks. Then she colored big dark black eyes. She colored a shirt the color of Fina's dirty shirt she was wearing. Fina colored Cristal's for her, drawing a ponytail and purple eyes. Fina didn't know her colors yet. She colored the shirt orange, but all out of the lines. The ponytail was pretty good though.

Next, they each had to recite the verse, "Jesus said, let the little children come to me, for of such is the kingdom of heaven." The pastora gave them a little bag of *churros* with hot sauce to eat. Cristal and Fina stuck their pieces of gum to the side of the bag until they finished the churros. They wanted to save it for later. The pastora looked at their pictures and smiled. She hugged them again and said they were little artists.

Cristal hated for the time to end. She felt like she was in real school. As the pastora was beginning to pick up, Cristal helped and then hesitantly asked if there were any other little jobs they could do around the church. The pastora smiled and said, "No, Cristal, we will be back Wednesday night though. Have a good week at school."

Cristal started to say something back, but she just smiled and thanked her for the churros. She and Fina walked home, with another long afternoon ahead of them. Sometimes she felt invisible.

Chapter 14

DANIEL

WHEN Daniel and his family got to the Hospital Infantil, Papá told Daniel to stay in the car and not get out for any reason. Mamá carried Memo, and the three ran to the emergency door. Daniel kicked the seat in front of him and cried angry tears. He was so tired of being left out and forgotten. *When was it his turn to be special?* He looked out the car window and saw the cool playground just behind the fence next door to the hospital. He wondered what kind of family lived there and got to play on all that fun stuff.

He looked around the car, reaching down into the back pockets of the seatbacks and under the seats. He found two of Memo's little race cars and began to play with them on the seat. When he tired of that game, he opened the console and the glove compartment and found three pesos. He knew that the last time they had been here, there had been a stand of churros right at the edge of the parking lot. One time when it was really cold, a lady had pulled up, opened her trunk, and given away free tamales and *champurrado* to all the families waiting to visit in intensive care! Free! That was great, but the scary Memo part was still too fresh in his memory. It wasn't too cold tonight. He walked over to the stand and bought a little bag of churros. The man let him add the hot sauce himself.

"Where's your mamá?" he asked Daniel.

"Inside with my little brother," Daniel answered.

"Where's your papá?"

"Inside too," he said. "They don't worry about me"

"Oh, I bet they just know they don't have to worry about you because you are a good boy. I bet they taught you how to take care of yourself," the man said.

Daniel looked at the man, thinking. He did know how to do lots of things. He could help his papá do stucco and block work and make change working at the *segundas*, well most of the time he did it right. He could read lots of books. He could even heat up a tortilla if Mamá lit the stove. And he always watched out for Memo. He watched Memo better than he had watched the scooter. Why was Memo sick again? Was God mad at him too for not watching the scooter? Daniel wandered back to the car and ate his churros. He tried not to think about Memo and the scooter. But he couldn't help it. *I bet Memo is scared.*

Then Papá came running out to the car. "Let's go," he said.

Papá didn't talk much. Daniel always had to ask him lots of questions to find out things. But Daniel was kind of scared to ask much tonight since Papá was already mad at him about the scooter, and now Memo was sick.

Finally, Daniel asked, "Is Memo spending the night?"

"Yes," said Papá with no more details.

They got home and went straight to bed. Daniel didn't ask for anything to eat. Before he drifted off, Daniel said a prayer, "Dear Lord, take care of Memo. I'm sorry I let my scooter get stolen. Don't take Memo away too just because I forgot to be careful."

Chapter 15

CRISTAL

W HEN Cristal and Fina got back home from the *comedor*, they played school a little with Aida, but soon Aida's mamá called her to go visit her *abuela*. Cristal remembered seeing her own *abuela* one time. She couldn't remember much except that she was a little scary. She wished she had a nice *abuela* to visit. She might put Cristal on her lap and read her books or tell her stories about when she was a little girl. Being on her lap would be like being on Jesus' lap, just like the story they heard at the *comedor* about Jesus spending time with the little children.

Later that afternoon a group of gringos came by with a young girl translating to them about the different block houses that were built in their neighborhood. She said Cristal's house was for a single mom with three kids, and the family was doing so much better now that they had a house. She described the pallet house, and all the gringos gasped and stared. Cristal felt funny inside.

The group moved on down the street and came to the work-site where they would begin to build another block house this week. The corners were marked, and the supplies would be delivered early in the morning. Cristal didn't know who would live there. She had never seen anybody in the little pallet house that was locked up in the middle of the site. The translator was telling the group that the family was probably out visiting family since that's what most Mexican families did on Sundays. "Most," thought Cristal.

She and Fina ate their apples and continued following the group. They would be at the site at 8:00am Monday morning with water bottles, work gloves, sunscreen, and hats. Then the team loaded into a van and left. It was kind of fun when a group was around. Sometimes they shared *chicle* or read stories. All alone, Cristal and Fina decided to walk to Daniel's house. Cristal had hoped Araceli would help her more with the alphabet, but no one was home. Disappointed, the girls headed home. It was getting dark, and they didn't want to run into Toño, so they began to run. But arriving home, the house was dark as Mamá had already gone out. Once again, the invisible girls were all alone.

Chapter 16

DANIEL

PAPÁ woke Daniel up early and told him to get ready to go. When he asked where, papá just grunted "hospital" without any more details. Daniel's eye hurt and for a minute he couldn't remember why. Then he remembered Toño, and he felt mad all over again. Daniel grabbed some books to read and some math practice sheets to help memorize times tables. He still needed to get his addition facts down too because Papá got mad if he saw him using his fingers.

They got in the car and drove to a burrito stand. Papá got 8 chorizo and egg burritos and a large Coke. They drove to the hospital as Papá ate three burritos and Daniel ate two. When they got to the *Hospital Infantil*, Papá ran in carrying the remaining burritos.

Once again Daniel waited in the car. He worked on his math facts and was reading a book when Mamá came out looking very tired. She hugged Daniel and thanked him for waiting in the car all by himself. But then she pulled his face up and cried, "Daniel, what happened to your eye?"

"It's nothing," said Daniel. "How's Memo?"

"It is something. Somebody punched you. What happened? Where were you? Was it here in the parking lot?"

"No," said Daniel, "Toño hit me."

"That Toño! I've told you not to play with him. Why are you having such a hard time minding us?" Mamá shouted. She took a deep breath and said, "Memo's on oxygen and having breathing treatments every four hours, but so far they are not putting him in to ICU," she said, exhausted from no sleep.

Mamá carefully drove them home. She was grateful for the old family car. It was more than 20 years old, but a few months earlier, a missionary helped them buy it. The generous man so how they suffered with transportation problems when Memo got sick suddenly. They were so thankful for this blessing in times of emergency.

Araceli did not have a license and had just learned to drive the last time Memo was so sick. Daniel remembered the policeman pulling them over when he and Mamá were on the way to the hospital the last time. She didn't have a license, and he didn't have on a seatbelt. Their old car didn't have any seatbelts that worked. She cried, and finally he agreed to let her go since they were so close to the hospital, but he gave them a stern warning. She still hadn't taken the test to get the license. She said it takes a whole day of waiting in line, and she just wasn't up to it. Daniel hoped they didn't get stopped again.

They made it home, and Mamá put in a load of clothes to wash making sure that the drainpipe was going into the shower. She made a little ice pack for Daniel's eye although it probably should have been done last night. Then Mamá began to cook some rice and beans, and pork in *chile verde*. Daniel went outside to find Aurora to play with. He had forgotten it was Sunday. He liked going to the Pastora's class at the *comedor*, but he was too late now. Aurora played a little bit until it was time for her to go visit her *abuelos*. Daniel came inside and asked to watch TV.

"Help me hang out the clothes first," Araceli said. "Then I need you to take the propane tank and refill it so I can finish cooking supper."

Daniel tried to hold in his groan. *Why did he have to do everything?* He helped tend the laundry and got the wrench to unscrew the tank. He walked the few blocks to the refill station. Taking it there was the easy part. Carrying it home was a lot harder. The man helped him hoist it up on his shoulders. As he walked off, he heard the man say, "What a strong little boy, and so responsible." Daniel walked a little lighter with pride, for a few steps. But it was heavy!

Daniel watched TV while Mamá finished cooking. "What about your homework? Tomorrow is Monday!" Mamá asked.

"I already did it," said Daniel "And I practiced my math facts in the car," he added.

Araceli stopped stirring for a minute and looked at her son. He was growing up so fast. She was so proud of him. "Thank you, *mijo*," she said and gave him a hug. They sat down and ate, saying a prayer together, thanking God for the food and asking for help for Memo. Then they packed up a big plate for Papá and headed out again to the hospital.

As they were coming in to the parking lot, Daniel saw a van turn in to the building beside the hospital with the letters DIF on it.

"What is DIF?" he asked.

"It's a place that takes care of children when their parents can't take care of them anymore."

Daniel watched as a lady helped three young children get out of the van and go into the building. They seemed to be crying. He wondered why they would cry when they were going to be staying where there was a great playground. "Why can't their parents take care of them?" he asked.

"Lots of reasons. Sometimes the parents are using drugs or drink too much. Sometimes they don't buy them enough to eat or don't take them to school. But no matter how bad the parents have been, it seems that the children still miss them. It's hard to understand how a parent wouldn't want to take the very best care of their children. It's sad." Then giving Daiel a quick hug, Mamá rushed in to the hospital with the hot plate for Papá.

Daniel thought about what she said. He slipped out of the car and went up to the fence to peek through. There was a big curving slide, swings, a merry-go-round, a bin full of balls, and a small soccer field with real goals with nets. He wished he could play there. He wished he lived there. But then he thought about it again and decided he really didn't want to live there. The playground at the neighborhood park had most of these same things, just not quite as new. Besides, who would cook for him and get him ready for school? Who would help with his homework? Would Memo get to go with him too? He thought about the three little kids he had just seen go inside. They didn't even have any toys with them. Had they had to leave everything behind?

"Daniel, get over here," shouted Mamá. He ran back as fast as he could, not wanting to get in trouble. "What were you doing over there?" she asked.

"I was just wondering what that would be like, living there," he said.

"Let's pray that you never have to find out," Mamá said. "Let's go. Papá is going to spend the night, and I'll come stay tomorrow night while he is at work."

"Where will I stay?" Daniel panicked.

"Either with *abuela* Elsa or *tía* Inés," Mamá said. "Who would you rather stay with?"

"I don't want to stay with *abuela* Elsa. She always yells at me, and sometimes we don't ever get anything to eat," Daniel said.

Araceli knew that her mamá's house was not a good place for Daniel to stay, but sometimes there wasn't a choice. "I'll see if *tía* Ines can keep you. But you might have to go home from school with *Abuela* first because I will already be at the hospital, and Papá will be at work." It was so complicated. Araceli worried about Daniel as much as about Memo. But Daniel was a good boy. He would make good choices. "God, watch over Daniel while we try to take care of Memo. And help Memo to breathe."

Daniel prayed for Memo too. He was an aggravating little brother who got all the attention, but he didn't want to be without him. And he didn't want to have to live in a DIF home either.

Chapter 17

DANIEL AND TOÑO

THE next week had a little routine for Cristal and Fina and also for Daniel. The gringo group was busy building the little block house, stopping sometimes for a break and sharing snacks with the girls. They asked lots of questions with their funny Spanish words, and the translator helped some, but Cristal tried to dodge most of them, not wanting them to know that she didn't go to school and couldn't read.

Daniel slept at *tía* Ines' house, and Papá picked him up early when he got off work at 6:00am. Then they drove to the hospital and brought Mamá some burritos. She came out and drove Daniel home while Papá tried to sleep in a chair beside Memo in the hospital ward with five other children and their mamás or papás. Mamá would do some chores and cook for the day, always fixing Daniel a snack for school. Then at one o'clock he went to school. Mamá took a nap and then went to the hospital in time to let Papá go back to work. When school was out, Abuela walked Daniel home until *tía* Ines could pick him up to spend the night. It was a crazy schedule, but it was working so far.

One afternoon at Abuela's house, Daniel was playing outside waiting on *tía* Ines. He was building a track for some of his cars out of scraps from other building projects in the neighborhood. He tried to keep the cars on his track as they raced down the strip of wood into a hole of water that he had dug. The gringo team had left for the day, and no one was around. Until Toño appeared.

"What you doin, Punk?" Toño dared Daniel to reply.

Daniel wanted to run, knowing his mamá didn't want him around Toño, but he couldn't act scared. "Nothing," he said, trying not to let his voice shake.

"Just playing with your little kiddie cars," Toño mocked.

Daniel didn't say anything back, but he stopped playing and slowly picked up the cars and wedged them into his pockets.

"Your papá can't buy you any big boy toys since he never goes to work," Toño said.

"He does too. He has a good job at a *maquila*," Daniel shouted.

Toño laughed and said, "Good one, Punk. I see his car at home all day. He's not working. You just think he is."

"He is too working. He works at night," Daniel cried out as he lunged at Toño. But Toño was bigger and quicker. He just dodged him and laughed at him some more.

"Go play with your kiddie cars, Punk. I don't have time to talk to babies."

Daniel ran inside trying not to cry. Abuela would not have any sympathy for him. He got out his backpack and worked on his homework, trying not to think about what Toño had said. *Did Papá really not have a job? Is that why they never had enough money?* The more he thought about it, the madder he got. *Why couldn't he have some pesos for snacks at school or afterwards walking home like the other kids? Why did he get yelled at about leaving the scooter out when Papá could go to work and buy one? Why did Daniel have to do everything when Papá was just home sleeping?* Thankfully *tía* Ines arrived with his cousins and he was able to get his mind off Toño's comments. But really, why couldn't he just be a kid like all his friends?

Chapter 18

CRISTAL

TODAY was the last day for the gringo team. Cristal and Fina enjoyed having something to do every day not to mention the snacks that the team shared with them. They hadn't gone to the dump all week. Cristal went by Daniel's house several afternoons, but no one ever came to the door. She was disappointed, but she was used to that. Nobody really cared about them.

The weather was warmer, and it seemed that the gringos liked to work out in the sun and turn brown. But some of them mostly turned red. She smiled remembering other teams before who had all gone home very sunburned.

One of the gringo girls began getting the translator to ask Cristal more and more questions. Cristal was a little worried because she was afraid the girl realized their mamá was almost never home. Then Cristal heard the dreaded word "DIF" as the translator tried to explain what can happen to neglected children. Cristal decided that maybe she and Fina should not hang around anymore with this team. Maybe another group would come next week.

Cristal called Fina to come with her. But Fina didn't want to miss out on the snacks or stories and activities. "No, Cristal," she yelled. "Not yet."

"Come on, Fina. We have to go," Cristal begged trying to make Fina understand with her expression. But, Fina wouldn't budge. Cristal decided to go alone, hoping Fina was too shy to say too much.

Cristal took the shortcut to the dump. She knew that once the team was gone, there would be nothing else to eat. She hoped the *comedor* would be open tomorrow, but she couldn't count on it.

The team of gringos had made them little bead bracelets and talked about the colors standing for things about this Jesus guy again, things such as life, snow, bad things, blood. *Why did they talk about blood so much? And what bad things had she done? She had tried to take care of Fina, tried to work to buy food and not steal it, tried to stay out of mamá's way and not make her mad. Why did she and Fina have to be washed in blood to be clean like snow?* It made no sense to her.

Plus, she was always hungry. *Why didn't they talk about that Jesus and the baskets of food and share some more of that? And where was the family that this house was for? Why were the gringos building for someone who didn't even live there?* She was so deep in her thoughts that she didn't notice Toño watching her from behind a broken plastic table. She stopped short and turned to run. But he was too quick.

"Where you going all by yourself, *gorda?*"

"Let me go, Toño," she said between clinched teeth.

"What's your hurry, *gorda?*"

"Let me go," she said louder.

"Where's your little baby boyfriend? Oh yeah, playing with his baby cars. Call for him now to come save you," Toño taunted her.

"Let me go, Toño!" she screamed louder as she heard footsteps. The team of gringos came running into the dump. But Toño was long gone.

"Are you all right?" they all asked at once.

"I'm fine," Cristal said shakily. "Really, I'm fine."

But the nosey member of the team said, "We have to do something. Come back to the site with us, and let's wait on our director."

"No," Cristal said. "We need to go home." She ran to Fina and grabbed her tightly by the hand, dragging her away toward home before she could protest this time. They slipped inside and hoped Ivan or Mamá would be home soon.

Chapter 19

DANIEL

SATURDAY morning Daniel and Papá went to the hospital hoping to pick up Mamá and Memo and bring them home. Daniel was excited. Maybe everything would get back to normal.

Daniel waited in the car in the hospital parking lot as Papá went in to check. He read his book and practiced math facts. It sure seemed to take them a long time.

It was getting hot in the car so Daniel decided to walk around some. There were other families waiting outside too. Some had slept on the sidewalks. He found some other boys near his age playing with some plastic rings they had found near the dumpster, throwing them up to a branch, seeing who could hook one the highest. It was something to do to break the boredom of waiting. Finally, he saw Mamá and Papá coming out slowly from the building, but Memo was not with them. Daniel ran as fast as he could to meet them.

"Where's Memo?" he cried. "Why didn't Memo come out?"

"Memo has to stay longer. He is not breathing well enough on his own. They put him back in ICU," said Mamá, trying not to cry. "They are going to give him stronger antibiotics and monitor his oxygen more closely."

"But why can't he come home? Why weren't they monitoring him more closely all this week?" Daniel was frustrated at a world he didn't understand.

"We just have to pray that God will continue to monitor him wherever he is and that the doctors will know what to do," said Mamá, trying to be strong. "We have to go home until the next visiting hour at six tonight."

"But, Memo is going to be all by himself all day?" cried Daniel incredulously. "How can he be monitored if his family is not there? I don't understand!" Daniel cried.

"I don't either," Mamá said so tired from the week of little sleep and no answers.

They drove home, Papá not talking but driving like a crazy man, racing past cars or up to their bumpers, honking and daring anyone to get in his way. They stopped at the Soriana for a few groceries and somehow made it home safely. Papá carried in the groceries and then busied himself under the hood of the car. Daniel asked Mamá if he could go to the *comedor*.

Araceli looked lovingly at her oldest son. "Yes, dear. Behave, and come home as soon as the activity is finished."

Daniel was running down the street when he heard Papá shouting at him, "Daniel, get back here. Where do you think you are running off to?"

"Mamá said I could go to the *comedor*," Daniel shouted in a disrespectful tone.

"Don't talk to me like that," Papá said. "Why do you need to go to the *comedor*? We just bought groceries."

"Why do you think you can tell me what to do when you don't even have a real job? And you can't even read!" Daniel shouted. He couldn't believe he said that, but it was out. He turned and ran. Papá's eyes looked so hurt. But Daniel kept running.

Chapter 20

PASTORA PATI

PASTORA Pati and her husband pastor Miguel had come to the *colonia* about two years ago. They both worked hard to keep their youngest child in the university and to have a little extra for their two grandchildren in the next *colonia* over. They decided to move here to try to make a difference, feeling God calling them to a new place. Their greatest desire was to serve God by making a difference in the lives of the most needy.

They had a small house and just a couple blocks over from the small church building with the *comedor*. There were some regular families each week, mostly women, but there didn't seem to be much life in the services. They wanted to get to know the families better, but the few who came just seemed to be checking off their attendance each week like some chore that had to be done. Their former church helped them provide meals for some of the children in the area who didn't often get much to eat.

Pastora Pati prepared the *comedor* for the meal and the activities for the day. She hoped the two little girls who seemed so lost would come today. She had fixed a special bag for each of them with a toothbrush, toothpaste, soap, shampoo, panties, socks, and some granola bars and fruit. She also had a children's Bible with great pictures that she hoped the oldest could read. She wanted to help, but she didn't know how. She prayed for the little girls every night, wondering how God could let these children just wander the neighborhood without anyone caring for them.

Soon the children began to arrive and she fixed them each a hot plate of rice, beans, chicken, and a fruit salad of mango, watermelon, papaya, and banana. At first the kids balked at the fruit salad, but she promised them *chicle* if they ate everything. Now they accepted everything and even asked for more fruit.

Pati hoped that they would like it more than all the candy and junk from the little stores on every corner. Although most of the children seemed to have enough to eat, she worried about their health. Most of them drank sugary drinks and ate sticky candies with *chile* all the time. She wanted them to make better choices and to take care of their bodies. She wanted them to be readers and finish school. She wanted them to be the best they could be for whatever life God had planned for each of them. But there were so many problems. Too many young mothers, too many adults with diabetes and high blood pressure, too many people without a future.

The two little girls came in last. She had learned their names Cristal and Fina, and knew where their house was, but she had never met the mamá. The story the pastora planned for today was about the paralyzed man who wanted to see Jesus. His friends took him, but it was so crowded that they couldn't get inside. The friends were so determined to help their friend that they took him to the roof, cut a hole, and lowered their friend down to Jesus. She wanted the children to think about how sometimes we have to sacrifice to help others, but she kept thinking that she and the other adults in the church should be sacrificing more to help others too. Her mind began to turn as she thought of ideas for helping Cristal and Fina.

Suddenly, Daniel burst through the door. He looked like he had been crying but was putting on a brave face.

"So glad you came, Daniel. Go ahead and fix you a plate. There is plenty left. Then come join us for the story," said the pastora. She wondered what had happened, but she didn't want to embarrass him. She told the story and asked the children to draw a picture of themselves helping a friend. For the ones who could write, she asked them to write about the picture. Then they would share their ideas. The children got busy, and she went to talk to Daniel who was still eating at the table.

"Are you ok?" she asked, also noticing what looked like the remains of a black eye.

"Yes," said Daniel, trying not to make eye contact.

"You know you can talk to me about anything?" the pastora said. "Did someone make you mad?"

"No," Daniel said and then, "Yes, my brother is the favorite, and all they want me for is to run errands and do chores, and now Memo is in intensive care again, and I'm mad at God because he didn't heal him like I prayed, and I let my scooter get stolen and now Memo is not coming home." Daniel sobbed, and the other children began to stare.

"Let's go outside Daniel and talk about it all," said the pastora.

When they got outside, she gently asked Daniel, "When did Memo get sick?"

"Last Saturday when I forgot and left my scooter outside, and it got stolen, and then God made Memo sick. I always look after Memo, but I just forgot the scooter for a minute and it was gone. Now God is punishing me by taking Memo away, and my papá has been lying about going to work, and he makes me do everything."

"Whoa, Daniel, let's slow down a little. I think maybe we need to clear up a few things. First, I'm so sorry that you lost your scooter. I'm sure you didn't mean for anything to happen to it. I don't think that God is punishing you for that. I bet your papá is just frustrated because he wants to help you be responsible, and I'm sure he worked hard to buy it for you."

"But he doesn't really go to work!" shouted Daniel, "Toño told me so."

"Oh, that Toño is always causing problems. You know sometimes we have to learn who we can trust, that's just part of growing up. God wants us to love everybody, but we still have to be on guard for 'snakes,' and I'm afraid that Toño is one of those snakes. God wants him to change, but right now, Toño is not listening to God. Which is a good reason for you not to listen to Toño either. Do you understand?"

Daniel nodded. He was remembering how Toño was always teasing him and aggravating him. He didn't know how to avoid him, or what to say when he came around. He made him so mad! Then he thought about Cristal and Toño and got mad again. "He's mean to Cristal too," he whispered.

"Thank you for letting me know that, Daniel. Did Toño have anything to do with that black eye?" she asked

Daniel nodded. He felt bad about what he had said to his papa. He was scared to go home. "What can I do?"

"Let's finish up here, and I will walk home with you," the pastora said. Then they went in, and several of the children shared some ideas about some small act that had helped their friends. One said that she shared her snack at school with a friend who didn't have any pesos for snacks. Another said that he read his reader book out loud to his little brother while his mamá was cooking. Another said that she had an aunt who brought her school supplies from the other side, and she shared them with a friend who didn't have any.

Then Cristal said, "I don't know what I can do, but someone ran off a bully who was trying to be mean to me. It was a sacrifice for him."

The pastora smiled. She was connecting the dots. "I so appreciate your good ideas. I'm going to challenge the grown-ups to think of what they can do too."

After the others had left, the pastora gave the bags to Cristal and Fina and hugged them. This time Cristal didn't tense up. Then Daniel and the pastora walked to his house.

When they got to the door, Daniel let the pastora knock and wait for Mamá and Papá to come to the door. They looked confused when they saw Daniel there.

"I wanted to come talk to you. Daniel told me that Memo is back in intensive care. I want you to know that we will be praying for him and for your family. I also want you to know what a wonderful son you have here. I'm not sure if you know exactly what happened with his black eye, but he was protecting a girl from a bully."

"Daniel, why didn't you tell us that's what happened. We thought you were just messing around with that Toño!" said Mamá as she grabbed him into a hug.

"I think that Daniel also has something to say to you," she said to Papá.

Daniel had to try a couple of times before the words came. Finally, he said, "Toño told me that you weren't really working, that you just made me do all the errands, and you didn't really want to work, and I'm sorry I listened to him, and I know he is just mean, I'm sorry," he sobbed, throwing himself into the open arms of Papá.

"I'd like to come pray for Memo at the hospital. When is the next visiting time?" the pastora said.

"Tonight at 6:00," Mamá said.

"I'll be there," she said. Quietly she left them to sort things out as she tried to sort things out herself including her ideas to share with her husband.

Chapter 21

LOS PASTORES

SATURDAY night, after returning from the hospital visit with Memo, Pastora Pati sat down to talk to her husband. He was preparing the sermon for tomorrow's service. He was a good man. He had worked on the other side when they first got married, faithfully sending home all his earnings. He had gone to English class at a church there learning English and and more. Before each class, the pastor shared a short devotional and little by little Miguel changed his way of thinking. God was no longer an idol, a statue. Miguel had God's spirit inside and he wanted to put God first in his life.

When Pati and Miguel decided to start a family, Miguel decided to find work in Mexico. He was no longer the typical macho man, and Pati was so thankful to him and to God for the change that only God could perform.

"Can we talk?" she asked. He smiled at her but didn't really want to stop what he was doing.

"Yes," he said patiently.

"I think that God is calling me, calling us, to do something more, something different. I'm tired of us telling the same Bible stories and listening to the same sermons and not seeing any change in our community," she said watching his face with caution as she spoke.

"What do you mean?"

"I think God is calling us to put this faith in to action and to challenge our group to come to action with us," she said softly.

"What did you have in mind?"

"I think we need to have a prayer meeting with our group in the morning, talking to each other about needs, their needs and needs in the community, and then brainstorm about how we can work together to help."

"What about my sermon and your music?"

"I think this week we should just turn off the sound and listen."

The pastor stared at his wife at first like she was an alien. *Maybe she was right. What had they really accomplished since they first came to this neighborhood?* They had a few faithful members, but he knew that they were lacking something, something more to attract more people and to see the change God wanted, true revival. He also wanted everyone to experience what he had come to understand. God didn't want memorized rituals. He wanted a personal relationship with each and every one.

Pati interrupted his thoughts with a question.

"When you were young, did you like to sit and listen to the pastor shouting scripture at you for over an hour? Why did we attend worship? Was it just another chore on our list?"

"I think so. Mamá always pulled me by the ear to get me there."

"OK, did you like the long, loud sermons you heard when you became a believer?"

"Well, no, but I thought that we had to endure it, like it was a requirement."

"Listen to this verse. I love this: *God has shown you what is good and what the Lord requires of you: act justly, love mercy, and walk humbly with God.*"

Miguel and Pati were both silent for a few minutes letting the verse sink in.

"But what will that look like? How do we act justly? love mercy? walk humbly? I know how the Holy Spirit changed me. He motivated me to want to share. But, I don't know how to make that feeling contagious."

"God will guide us. It shouldn't be so complicated. We have to remember the two greatest commandments of love God and love our neighbor. Just like the ones who showed us mercy when we were finding our way, we can do the same," Pati said.

"But shouldn't we have some kind of plan before we just jump out there with this idea?"

"Well, I do have a starting point. We have the family with the young boy in the hospital. We could organize some food for them or offer to help with getting the other boy to school. And then there are the two girls I've told you about before," Pati said as she thought of the tremendous need everywhere in their small community.

"But won't these families just think we are being nosey, in their business?"

"They might at first, but that is where prayer comes in. With God's help I believe that we can make a difference in those families and in the lives of the families who agree to help."

"Let's pray about it now," he said and smiled at his wife, his amazing helpmate.

Chapter 22

A NEW START

SUNDAY morning brought awful winds, carrying clouds of dirt, making little whirlwinds around the neighborhood. The pastora brought a small cd player and set it up in the rustic chapel, softly playing some Christian music. The pastora carried the snacks she had prepared to the small *comedor*. Then they headed out on foot in the swirling dust to the homes of the faithful few to invite them to a different service this morning.

They stopped by Aida's house and invited both her parents, asking Aida to try to make sure that Cristal and Fina came. They stopped by Daniel's house, but Araceli said they needed to leave at 11:00 to get to the hospital for visiting hours. Araceli said she would try to come to church for a little bit. They also invited Aurora's mamá from the little store next door and a few others who had visited before. There was a family whose father worked some in construction on the other side and was a good singer, a family whose papá worked as a plumber and electrician, but his wife struggled with alcohol, and a family whose mamá was a beautician and the papá was a policeman on the night shift. No perfect families, but each one persevering bravely. All said they would come.

Finally, about 10:00am, many of the families gathered even with the dirt flying. Maybe they were just curious. They also were surprised that there was no blaring music and jokingly asked if the power was turned off. The children stayed in the *comedor*, colored some pages, and did some puzzles while the adults met. The pastor asked them to sit in a circle, opened with prayer for direction, and began to explain what he and his wife had discussed the night before.

"I've been a pastor for about five years now. I have never studied at a seminary. I have only copied what I have seen. But last night my wife asked me if there might be another way. She asked me to read a verse in Micah with her. I didn't want to listen at first, but God spoke to me too. He made me see the many needs in our community.

Then we read from the book of James which said that our faith should produce good works. We should want to help our neighbor, not to earn our way to heaven but as a way to show gratitude to God. How can I say I love the Jesus I can't see, but not show compassion for the neighbor I can see? Our faith without works is dead. James challenges us to put our love into action.

"How is my shouting the same sermons each week making a difference in our people? Jesus never shouted his message. How is just teaching Bible stories to our children enough? Jesus didn't just teach in the synagogue. He was out doing something with the people, doing miracles! What about putting our faith and those stories into action? How can we bring our faith to life?"

He stopped talking as he looked at his friends and neighbors, and let some of what he said sink in. Then he told a little about what his wife had asked the children at the *comedor* the day before about small sacrifices to help another. He asked how the church might help each of them, and how they as a church could help their community.

There was silence at first as they tried to grasp what they were hearing. No one wanted to ask for help. There was too much pride. So, the pastora said, "I know it is different and hard to open up to each other. There is always so much gossip among us that we don't know who to trust. I think maybe first we need to have an agreement, a pact, that we will not discuss anything with anyone else outside of the church. If someone has a need, we will help without telling anyone about it." Many shook their heads in agreement. It was hard not to gossip. What else was there to talk about in this neighborhood? Gossip was the main hobby for most of them.

Then Aurora's mamá said, "I have a big problem at the store with a boy trying to take things. I think his name is Toño. He always tries to distract me by teasing Aurora. Then when I take care of her, he grabs something and runs. Is that the kind of thing you mean?"

"Yes, exactly, thank you," said the pastora. "That's exactly what I mean. Let's talk about Toño and see how we might help. Let's just remember that we will not talk about any of this outside of here. Let's not let the left hand know what the right hand is doing."

Araceli excused herself and left for the hospital. The pastora told the others that they could also think of ways to help Araceli while Memo was in the hospital. But first, they discussed Toño.

"I always just try to scare him with my badge and uniform," said the policeman smiling.

"But he doesn't seem scared of that," said the policeman's wife. "Where are his parents?"

No one seemed to know for sure. Aida's papá said that they lived past their house. "I think his papá works driving a truck and is gone for days at a time. His mamá just can't control him, and he has been kicked out of school."

"Maybe he needs a job."

"Maybe he needs to go to the juvenile detention."

"He should have gotten the belt a long time ago."

Everyone knew Toño. He had been a problem for a long time, but now he was getting older and becoming a bigger problem. The pastora sadly thought about what they should have been doing. But then she said, "We can't change the past, but we can help make the present better. Who would like to go with me to talk to his mamá?"

Aida's mamá said, "I can go. I don't know how to help, but I can go support you."

"Thank you," said the pastora. "Now, who can share a dish of food with Araceli this afternoon when they return from the hospital?"

Aurora's mamá quickly volunteered. Then the pastora said, "Thank you for a good start. I'm also concerned about these two little girls, Cristal and Fina."

Aida's mamá responded, "There's also a brother Ivan."

"I didn't know that. Where does he stay?"

The policeman answered, "My friend in the next *colonia* is a mechanic. Ivan hangs out with him, helping in his shop."

The pastor said, "Could you go with me to meet Ivan and your friend?"

Soon some simple plans were coming together. They prayed that God would guide them and promised to meet again Wednesday night to see how things were going. The pastora went to the comedor with the children, and this time Aida's mamá and Aurora's mamá stayed to help. The policeman even asked if he could play soccer with them after their activity. The fellowship and planning had been the best worship time in a long time, maybe the best ever. It was a good morning.

Chapter 23

DANIEL

WHEN Daniel's parents got to the noon visiting hour, Memo was sitting up and breathing on his own. Mamá and Papá were relieved. Hopefully Memo could go home on Monday. Daniel hated to think of his brother staying all by himself in there. It didn't seem fair and was more than a little scary

But Memo didn't come out with Mamá and Papá. He would spend another night alone. Daniel could see the worry on Mamá's face, so he worried too.

As they drove home, Mamá talked a little about what was said at the church this morning. Careful not to gossip, but wanting to help, she asked Daniel more about Toño.

"He's a bully. He has always pestered me, but now he is just being mean to me and to Cristal."

"Why can't he go to school?" asked Mamá.

"He can't read!" said Daniel. "He is stupid."

"Daniel, not everybody who can't read is stupid! Plus, you know not to use that word." said Mamá sternly. "There is probably a good reason why he can't read." She didn't know why her husband couldn't read either, but he was not stupid! He could handle all the money and knew how much material to buy for building projects. He wasn't stupid!

Daniel hung his head, and they rode on in silence to the house. When they got home, Aurora's mamá was waiting with a pan of rice and a plate of flautas with lettuce and Mexican cream on top. What a nice surprise!

"*Gracias, vecina!*" they all said. The two mamás hugged each other.

"How is your *hijo*?" she asked.

"We hope he can come home tomorrow," said Mamá.

They sat down to eat, prayed a prayer of Thanksgiving, and asked for help for Toño and Memo. But, one bite in and they immediately got a call from the hospital. Memo was being moved to a regular room, and someone had to come be with him right that minute. They wolfed down the food and zoomed off in the car. They would decide who would stay when they got there.

Chapter 24

PASTORA

PASTORA Pati and Aida and her mamá walked slowly to Toño's house. They called at the gate, tapping a rock on the pallet post and calling *buenas tardes.* A scary dog was chained beside the entrance and began to bark and growl. Just as they were about to leave, Toño came up the street.

"Nobody's home."

They stared at Toño, realizing how big he had gotten since they last saw him.

"Where's your mamá?" the pastora said.

"She's gone to take care of my *abuela.*"

"When will she be back?"

"Maybe *mañana.*"

"And your papá?"

"I don't know."

They didn't believe him but had no ideas.

"Toño, do you need anything?" the pastora said.

"My papá takes care of me," he said angrily.

They shrugged and walked back to the church. They would need a man to help with this situation.

The children were just finishing a fun game of soccer with the policeman being coach and referee.

"Pastora, these girls are good players. Maybe we could form a girls' soccer team. Maybe we could play a team in the next *colonia.*"

The pastora smiled as she saw the excited faces of the girls, even Cristal saying, "Sí, sí" along with the rest.

"I think that is a great idea. Why can't girls have a team? But now, could you go with the us to try to find Ivan? I'd like to talk to you about Toño too."

The policeman agreed, and the children helped pick up the *comedor*. She thanked the women, and one by one they went with their children back to their houses. Cristal and Fina left in another direction moving the slowest of all.

Chapter 25

DIF

CRISTAL and Fina went back to their house with their special bags from the pastora. They were happy and full. They talked about where they would hide their things and sang parts of the songs they were learning. They rounded the corner of their house just as a DIF van pulled up. The girls froze. Where was Mamá? Where was Ivan? Cristal grabbed Fina's hand and started to bolt off, but a man in a white shirt with DIF written on it jumped out and grabbed them both.

"Where you going, miss?" he said. "Not so fast, where is your mamá?"

"I don't know," Cristal said in a low voice.

"We need you two to come with us," he said, and the girls began to cry. He put them in the van and shut the door. The doors had child guard locks; they could not open them from the inside. A lady was driving, but she didn't even acknowledge them. She pulled out heading for who knew where.

Chapter 26

POLICÍA

T HE policeman's name was Jesús, but everyone had always
called him Chuy. Now most of the kids called him *poli,* a
nickname for policeman. He thought he would like also being
known now as the coach of the girls' soccer team.

Chuy was the youngest of ten children. He had grown up
in another colonia nearby and still visited his mamá every Sunday afternoon. He would have to be a little late today. Since
becoming a papá himself, he realized how incredible his mamá
really was. How had she raised ten of her own and still had
time to invest in other kids' lives in the neighborhood? With
just two kids, Chuy and his wife were always busy.

Remembering his childhood, Chuy thought about his papa.
He had never hit his mamá and had kept a steady job, but mamá
was the one who kept them all together. All of his siblings had
finished *secundaria* with two finishing *prepa* and one graduating
university. And each one of them had felt like he or she was
Mamá's favorite. He remembered how proud she was when he
graduated the police academy.

Chuy lost his papá a couple of years ago to complications
from diabetes and alcohol. His mamá carried on. She often
talked to him about how to help the young people in the *colonia*
stay away from the drugs and gangs and how to keep the girls in
school and not get a pregnant belly at age 13. She really worried

about her own grandchildren too. There seemed to be more gang violence, and although she didn't understand social media she knew it could be a tool of the devil.

Chuy walked with the pastor toward his friend Jairo's house. Jairo had grown up next door to him. Jairo's parents weren't around much, but Chuy's mamá invited him to their full house. With her support, Jairo had finished *secundaria* and learned enough about cars to open a little *taller mecánico* right on the street in front of his house. Starting out with used tools from the *segundas*, Jairo had slowly replaced them with better quality as he got more business. A cool dude from the other side had stopped one day to see Jairo work and given him a new set of socket wrenches. About once a year the man would appear and give Jairo another new gadget, like the computer diagnostic scanner to see what was malfunctioning in the engine. Even though Chuy had moved to a new *colonia*, he and Jairo had remained friends. They didn't talk a lot, but they did realize that God had blessed them both in a rough area where many kids didn't make it out.

As Chuy and the pastors neared Jairo's house, they could hear music coming from the house where Chuy grew up. It was praise music. Chuy knew that his mamá was having her own church today at home. Most of his nieces and nephews would be coming by soon, and she would have a big pot of *pozole* cooking or maybe *tamales*. Jairo was sitting on the patio in the *sombra* at his house. He waved them over, and Chuy made the introductions, telling him the reason for the visit. Ivan was a good example of the type of kid Chuy's mama liked to help. For that reason, Jairo had quickly jumped in to help.

"Ivan is a great kid. He learns fast! He can change the oil faster than I can and is already diagnosing problems with just a little information. I just sent him to the store to get us a Coke."

"Do you know anything about his family?" Pastor Miguel asked.

"He never talks about them, but he is always hungry!" laughed Jairo. "I try to feed him well while he is here, and your mamá helps out as always. What would I have done without her help when I was Ivan's age?"

The pastora smiled and said, "We are really worried about his little sisters. They just wander the neighborhood all day, always hungry too, and more vulnerable than Ivan."

"I didn't even know he had sisters."

"And there is a boy who is causing us worry, especially in relation to these girls. His name is Toño. Do you happen to know him?"

Jairo frowned and said, "I think he is the one who beat up Ivan before Ivan started coming here. A big tall kid?"

"Yes, probably the same one. We just don't know how to help him. Any ideas?" asked the pastora.

"Well, I know we want to save them all, but sometimes some of them are so hardheaded that only the *tribunal* can get their attention. I'm doing all I can for Ivan. I don't want Toño over this way when I just got Ivan to trust me. I'll see what else I can find out about Ivan's family and let you know if I can help more that way. Be careful of that Toño though. He's probably a tough one."

Chapter 27

PASTORA

PASTORA Pati was driving to the hospital hoping to make it in time to see Daniel's parents and be able to go in to ICU to pray over Memo. What a long day! She was so happy with the response of the church this morning, but even more happy about the response of her husband last night. For a Mexican man to listen to an idea from a woman and much less his wife had to be because God was working. And for Chuy to step up to help too was incredible. Now they had another connection with the brother of the girls, another part of the body of Christ working to help the lost.

She pulled in to a parking spot beside the *Hospital Infantil* and immediately saw Daniel running toward her crying.

"What is it? Where are your papás? Tell me what's wrong"

"They just took Cristal and her sister," he sobbed. "They took them inside that DIF building and wouldn't let me talk to them."

Pastora held him tight, looking at the DIF building and desperately trying to think of what to do. "Where are your papás?"

"Inside with Memo."

"Stay here and let me see what I can do." And "Lord help me," she prayed silently.

Pastora knocked at the DIF building entrance. After a long wait, a young man cracked open the door.

"No one is allowed inside."

"I would like to speak to a supervisor about helping out with the two little girls who just came into care."

"No one is allowed inside."

"I don't have to come inside! Please, can you go get your supervisor in charge tonight?"

The young man closed the door, and pastora Pati waited. She could see Daniel walking dejectedly on the sidewalk in front of the hospital. It was getting dark, and the hospital visitors were beginning to leave. Finally, she heard some movement behind the DIF door. It opened, and a woman about her same age looked out.

"I'm pastora Pati from the church in the *colonia* where the two girls live who were just brought in, Cristal and Fina. I wanted to know if our church could help to keep these girls at home."

The supervisor looked very tired. Her clothes were wrinkled from being on duty since Friday night. The long weekend shifts were exhausting. She was just counting the minutes until the next worker came on duty. She didn't know what would happen to those poor girls.

"I'm sure you know that I cannot tell you who is here or anything about their cases. You will have to go to the DIF main office tomorrow morning to file a request for information. The judge will have to decide if you are considered a familial contact or not."

The official bureaucratic talk did not deter the pastora. "I'm sure you have more than the number of children staying here allowed by law. I'm sure you have probably been on duty longer than is acceptable by childcare standards. And I'm sure that allowing two little girls to go stay in a loving home with food and resources would lighten the load of everyone involved here. Who told you to go make the pick-up on a Sunday night anyway?"

The supervisor sighed. "There was an American lady making a lot of noise at the border as she was leaving about the terrible conditions that our government was allowing our Mexican children to grow up in. The children were already on our radar, but the higher ups said to go get them tonight."

"Our church wants to take them in. They can stay with me and my husband, and the families in our church are going to make sure that they have food and clothes. We want to get them in to school too as soon as they have learned some basics. Can I at least see them? I don't want them to think they can't trust me or that I had anything to do with this."

"OK, but just for five minutes. Then tomorrow go to the main DIF office downtown to start the process."

Driving home that night the pastora thought about what a different Sunday she had had compared to her other more "worshipful" Sundays. She thought of the verse that they had studied, "What does the Lord require of you? To love justice, to show mercy, and to walk humbly with your God." And the realization that the burnt offering sacrifices were not what God required, and not interminably long worship services either, but instead the sacrifice it takes to love Him and to love our neighbors. Wasn't that more important than which songs to sing, and wasn't it more effective than her husband shouting Bible verses into a microphone? She couldn't wait to get home to talk to Miguel. Memo was on the way home tomorrow and hopefully Cristal and Fina would be too.

Pastora Pati passed Chuy on his motorcycle on his way to his night shift. He worked Sunday through Thursday 8pm to 8am. She prayed for safety for him and for others in the neighborhood as she drove through. She prayed for Aurora's family as she passed their little store. She prayed for Aida's family as she passed down the street where Cristal and Fina also lived. She didn't see Ivan, and no lights were on. She finally made it home and said a prayer of thanks, asking for guidance for tomorrow.

Chapter 28

DIF

CRISTAL and Fina were together in a tiny bed. They had only slept in a real bed the other time they were in a DIF house. This one seemed a little nicer. They ate a quesadilla for supper and drank a glass of milk. Scared, sad, and anxious, they were grateful for full stomachs.

Suddenly, the pastora appeared. The girls were so glad to see a familiar face they hadn't even hesitated to run and hug her. She promised them she would do everything she could to get them out. She said they hadn't done anything wrong, that God would take care of them. She asked about Ivan, but Cristal didn't know what to tell her. Pastora hadn't even bothered to ask about her mamá since they never seemed to count on her. She asked them to behave and reminded them again of God's protection over them. Then she was gone.

Cristal wanted to be hopeful. They would get out soon. Even though they didn't have a loving home, it was the only home they had known. She wanted to trust the pastora, but she knew adults didn't keep their promises She was glad to be away from Toño, but there were other scary kids here too.

Cristal kept Fina with her every second, even when they were told to bathe. They missed their house, but not the conditions. Here they had hot water and clean clothes.

After their bath and hair-washing, the woman poured some awful-smelling stuff on their heads to kill the lice and nits. She said they would comb it all out tomorrow. Cristal and Fina clung to each other, climbed into bed, and soon Fina fell asleep. Cristal kept thinking about the soccer game at church and the nice policeman who wanted to start a girls' team. She hoped they got out of there so she could play. She could be a star. Maybe even her mamá would watch. She fell asleep dreaming of making a goal.

The next morning there was a new DIF lady waking them up and shouting for them to get dressed and go to the *comedor*. Cristal and Fina hurried with the rest and ate the small bowl of cereal and milk. Then the new lady took Cristal and Fina outside to comb out their nits. She was not gentle, and Fina began to cry.

"We'll have to cut it all off if you're gonna keep crying. Stand still and get it over with," she snarled.

The girls just stared at each other and held hands. The lady poured some oil all over their scalps and rubbed it in. It smelled ok but felt greasy. Maybe it would stop the itch though. They went to the TV room until something could be decided about their schooling.

"What's that smell?" A surly boy about the age of Toño glared at them.

Cristal just ignored him. She hoped the pastora would come soon. But lunchtime passed, and still they waited.

Chapter 29

DANIEL

DANIEL woke up in his own bed with Memo kicking his foot. He smiled at that for a change. He was glad Memo was home. He jumped up in a good mood and got out his backpack. He wanted to have everything ready for school so if Papá wanted to play, he would be ready.

With a happy face, Daniel asked Mamá if he could help her with anything. She gladly sent him to buy tortillas at the little store, and he bounced out the door, relieved that his family was back together again.

The little store hadn't opened yet, but soon he heard the sound of the motorcycle that came by selling tortillas off the back from a foam chest that kept them warm. He flagged the guy down and paid for his kilo of tortillas. They were fresh from the store, and still hot. Mamá would be pleased. But as he turned to go home, he saw Toño.

Toño was just jumping down from the back window of the store next door. He had a heavy backpack and a guilty face. As soon as his eyes met Daniel's, Daniel knew there would be trouble. He wanted to run, but it was hopeless.

"Don't Toño," he tried to scream, but Toño was too quick.

He grabbed Daniel and put his hand over his mouth pulling his ear up to his mouth as he hissed, "You say a word about seeing me, and your little girlfriend will be another scrap in the dump." Then he punched Daniel so hard in the stomach that Daniel couldn't breathe. He tried to pull away, but Toño pushed him to the ground. He was about to stomp on Daniel's head when they both heard another motorcycle. Daniel knew it was Chuy, and he would be safe. Toño started to run, but Chuy skidded to a stop and tackled him, pulling Toño's hands behind him and handcuffing him in an instant.

"You just won't listen, Toño. This isn't the way. Daniel, you ok? Can you make it home?"

Daniel nodded, picked up his dirty bag of tortillas, and walked shakily back home.

Chapter 30

PASTORA

PASTORA Pati was up early as usual, getting her husband off to his shift at the maquila with a hot breakfast and some burritos for break time. She drove him to work and returned home to finish wrapping the last of her usual 100 tamales to sell at her morning stand. She hoped to finish quickly and be able to get to the DIF office before noon.

Last night she and her husband had discussed what to do with the girls. They had enough room to take them in, but they didn't know what problems the mamá might cause. No one seemed to know about the papá. She wondered if the mamá might be home now, would she even be wondering where her girls were, and would she even care.

About noon, Pastora Pati was finishing her tamale sales and packing up her things when a young woman called out in her direction.

"Hey, what have you done with my kids?"

"Can I help you?" asked the pastora. The woman appeared to have just gotten out of bed still wearing pajama pants but with a low-cut lacy black blouse. Her hair was sticking up in several places.

"My kids are missing, and it's your fault. Where are they?"

"Are you Cristal and Fina's mamá?"

"You know who I am. Where are my kids? You don't need to be messing around in my life. They are none of your business."

"What's your name?" the pastora tried to tread lightly.

"Just get my kids," she said more loudly.

"I don't have your children, but DIF does. Well, DIF has the girls. I don't know about your son. I didn't know about him until yesterday. How can I help you?"

"You're the one who called DIF so don't go talking so sweetie to me!"

"No, I'm not the one who called," but she was interrupted by the woman shouting at her.

"Yes, you are. I saw the bags of things you gave them. What business are they of yours? Those are my kids. Leave them alone!"

"They are your children, but they are my responsibility too. They are precious in God's sight," said the pastora adding softly, "just like you."

"God doesn't have a thing to do with us, never has!" she shouted.

"I think he has done more than you realize. But He can do a lot more if you will let us be the way. We, our church, with God's help, we want to help."

"I don't need your help!" shouted the mamá even more furiously.

"Mamá, you do. And your children do. Let us help. I'm on the way to the DIF right now to try to help. Please let me."

"Stay out of my business!" she yelled again.

"Señora, please help yourself by accepting that you need help. Or if not for yourself then for your children. They are the ones suffering in this situation. Let us help you and help resolve the girls' DIF case. I'm on the way to the DIF office now. I want to see what I can do to help them."

"Get out of my business! I don't need anybody feeling sorry for my kids." She stomped off in the direction of the DIF office.

Pastora Pati finished packing up and wanted to drop everything at her house. Instead, she went straight to the DIF office as fast as she could. When she entered the main waiting area, the girls' mamá was already there waiting too.

"What are you doing here?" she snarled.

"I care about your girls," said the pastora.

A social worker opened a door and called, "Rubí Mendoza."

The girls' mamá jumped to her feet and demanded, "Where are you keeping my kids?"

Before the social worker could answer, pastora Pati intervened, "Excuse me, I am Rubí's pastor and am here to help. Could we come in to your office to talk?"

The social worker opened the door wider and directed them to a tiny, dingy office. Rubí did not know how to respond to Pati's interference.

"Cristal and Fina attend our church regularly and are very sweet girls. I'm sure there has been some kind of misunderstanding. We, I mean our church, my husband is the pastor, we want to support Rubí and the girls while they get on their feet," the pastora struggled to explain.

Rubí didn't want any help, and she sure didn't want any church help. She started to say so, but then decided to bite her tongue.

The social worker looked at Rubí and asked, "Is this true? Is this your church?"

Rubí looked down and mumbled, "Maybe my kids go some."

"Would you be willing to allow the church to help you get on your feet?"

Rubí didn't want anything to do with this plan, but she didn't know how else she would get her kids out. "Yeah, sure."

"What is your church willing to do?" the social worker asked.

"My husband and I can keep the girls while Rubí looks for a job. The families in our church are willing to help. And we would like to help Rubí too, maybe with some food, house repairs, and if she is willing, a stay in a drug rehab program."

"I don't need your help," hissed Rubí, growing angry again.

"I suggest that if you want to see your girls you try to cooperate with us," the social worker said.

Rubí lowered her eyes, but the pastora could feel her anger. "Could the girls come stay with us until a decision has been made instead of staying at the DIF house? I'm sure you are always in need of more beds," the pastora said, trying to kill her with kindness.

The social worker looked at her with tired eyes and said, "Yes, we always are. Let me come by and see your house, and I think we can make this work. What time will your husband be home? I'll need to meet him too."

Pastora Pati and the social worker made arrangements to meet at Pati's house at 6:00pm, and Rubí was invited to be there also. "Remember that we are all trying to help," said the social worker.

"I said I don't need your help or anyone's! And like DIF ever helped anybody. You two just talking about my kids like I'm not even here. Give me a break. Those are my kids, and I don't need anybody telling me how to raise them." Rubí was gaining steam again. She had been in DIF as a child. She knew the horrors of those homes. "I want my kids out now!"

"Ms. Mendoza, I need you to calm down and work with us on this. This might be your last chance to get it right."

Rubí stormed out of the office and slammed the door.

Chapter 31

THE PASTORS

C HUY had taken Toño to the *tribunal* for youthful offend-
ers. He hated leaving the boy there, but he didn't know
any other options. It was his job. Toño had a backpack full
of stolen items besides beating up Daniel. Chuy caught a ride
back to his motorcycle and walked it home. He told his wife
Nilda about his night, and then remembered about Daniel. His
wife told him to go to bed. She would check on Daniel and call
the pastora.

Pastora was just getting home when she realized that her
phone was silenced since being at the DIF office. She redi-
aled the missed call as she quickly began organizing her house
for two precious little girls. She hoped she wasn't getting her
hopes too high. Then she listened as Nilda told her about Toño,
his stolen property, and the assault on Daniel.

Once again Pati wondered why their church hadn't tried
to help before? She reminded herself it was water under the
bridge. Now they had the chance to save two little girls, and
they wouldn't be found lacking this time. Jairo had wisely said
they couldn't save them all. But they could sure jump in and
try their best this time. She promised God she would give her
best effort.

"Do you have time to check on Daniel?" the pastora said
Nilda.

"Yes, I don't have any appointments. I'll run over there now."

"Ok, and I will ask Miguel to try to find Toño's parents when he gets off work. Also, if you can spread the word, we are hoping that the girls Cristal and Fina will be staying here with us for a while, and we will need some things for them."

"I'll let Araceli know, but only people in our group for now, right?"

"Yes, I think that is best."

Pastora Pati looked at their tiny house. Their son's twin bed would need some clean sheets and some privacy. She took the sheets off the bed and formed a kind of tent wall around the bed using some string from Miguel's tool box. She got her only other set of sheets and made the bed. She found a plastic bin for them to keep their clothes in and to serve as a side table. Then she checked the little bathroom and found only one extra towel. She hoped they still had the little bags of toiletries that she had given them.

She admitted to herself she would have to ask the other families for help with sheets and towels and probably some clothes. Maybe some help with food too. She would have to get over that shamed feeling of having to ask for help. She was sure the others felt the same. Maybe her asking would be an example to the others. Why were they that way? Pride? Shame? Were those really the same words? Two sides of a coin? The girls had to come first. She would focus on the inspection first, then ask for help, not just a general request, but specific needs.

Pastor Miguel got home just as the DIF social worker drove up. He was tired from being on his feet, handling sheets of plastic molding all day. Pati had not been able to fill him in on anything and asked the social worker for just a minute alone. Pati and Miguel went inside to catch up as the social worker began a look around the yard and got an idea of the neighborhood. She had seen lots of cases, many much worse than this file. Pati and Miguel were coming out of the house smiling when suddenly Rubí appeared obviously under the influence of something. Her eyes were red and she couldn't walk in a straight line.

"Where are my kids?" she screamed, attempting to run toward the social worker.

"Stay back, Ms Mendoza. You are not helping your case."

"You can come in now," said Pati holding the door. But Rubí was right behind.

Pastor Miguel stepped in to try to calm the situation. "I'm pastor Miguel, Pati's husband. We want to help. Please let us help you and your girls."

"I don't need your help. I need my kids back. They are mine," she tried to yell, but her speech slurred.

"Listen, Rubí," said pastor Miguel. "We want to help. We want to help you take care of your girls. We can take care of them here where you can easily see them every day. If DIF keeps them, you can only see them at certain times. But right now, we would not let you see them either because you are under the influence of something. You can't be a mother to them in this condition. Let us help you."

Rubí started to swing her fist but lost her balance and stumbled against the social worker's car.

"Please go home and sleep this off. You can come back later and maybe the girls will be here," pastora Pati said, looking at the social worker with hope in her eyes.

"Let me walk you home," said Pastor Miguel.

But Rubí just stomped off down the street, weaving as she went.

The three went inside for the home inspection. The social worker admired the patience and respect the pastors had shown Rubí. She had dealt with angry mamás before and knew how hard it was not to react in the face of such angry emotions.

"I'm impressed with how both of you treated Ms Mendoza. I wish we had more couples like you for our DIF children. I'm going to see if we can bring the girls tonight if you are ready."

"Would it be possible for me to pick them up?" Pati asked.

"I feel sure. Thank you. I'll call as soon as I know."

Then papers were signed, and Pastor Miguel and Pastora Pati were ready and excited to pick up the girls from DIF. A little anxious too, but ready.

After the social worker left, Miguel decided they should go by Toño's house again while waiting for the call. He hoped to find someone home at this time of night.

Miguel found the house and avoided the big dog still tied outside. He knocked at the gate, but no one responded. He was about to give up when he heard a truck approach and park. A large man in a sweaty hat got out with a tall bottle of beer in his hand. "Who you looking for?"

"Are you Toño's papá?" asked the pastor.

"What's he done now? Who are you? Why can't people mind their own business?"

"I'm pastor Miguel and this is my…"

"We are not interested in your little handouts. Get on out of here."

"We aren't here with handouts, sir. Toño is at the *tribunal*. We wanted to let someone know."

"His mamá better be back tomorrow to take care of that. Now go on. It's none of your business," he waved his beer can at them as he spoke.

"When will she be home?"

"I said it's none of your business," he shouted this time, his hands a little shaky as he tried to get his door open to the block house. The big dog couldn't reach him because of his chains, but a hungry chihuahua ran around his feet. He kicked at it as he went inside.

Miguel went back to the car where Pati waited. On to their next mission. They were excited for the girls but sad for Toño. How did any of these kids ever make it out?

Chapter 32

CRISTAL AND FINA

A long afternoon passed by at DIF. Even though Cristal and Fina watched TV, looked at books, and did a few puzzles with missing pieces, they weren't used to being inside so long without walking the streets. About 4:00 they were given a snack of a slice of papaya. It reminded them of the pastora. *Why hadn't she come?* They tried to be patient and optimistic since she had promised to return. By 7:00 all the kids were back from school or some other activity. Cristal and Fina tried to remain invisible to all of them but especially to the bully. Unfortunately, the older boy managed to find them and began to pester them.

"Gross! What's that greasy stuff on your head?" he laughed pointing and nudging his buddies to join in.

"At least we have hair. They must have had to shave off all your nits," snapped Cristal just as the woman in charge for the night came in.

"Girls! Get to your side of the room, and stop talking to the boys. We have rules here. Girls on one side, boys on the other."

Fina started to say something back, but Cristal hushed her with a hard glare and whispered, "Remember what Pastora said."

Supper was a plate with a cold taco of some kind with rice and beans and a baby cup of watery juice. They ate quickly. Then the lady told them it was their turn to do chores. They collected the plates, scraped and stacked them, and wiped off the tables. Then they swept under the tables and took out the trash. Outside the two girls whispered to each other.

"Why didn't pastora Pati come?" asked Fina.

"She probably forgot. We can't count on anybody else. You know that."

"Yeah, but she promised."

"Lots of grown-ups make promises."

"When are we going home?"

"Maybe never. Just don't say anything to anybody, especially that big boy. He is just waiting to cause us trouble."

"Hurry up, *chicas!*" the big boy shouted at them from the door. "you have more work to do. Come mop this floor, and then clean this bathroom off the kitchen."

"Nobody said to do that," shouted Fina, forgetting what Cristal had told her.

"I told you, and if you don't want trouble tonight, you better get in here now."

The girls looked around for the lady, but she was nowhere in sight.

"She's not here," grinned the boy. "She has her smoke break now, so I'm in charge."

Seeing no alternative, Cristal went into the little storage area to get a mop bucket. She didn't realize the boy followed her in, blocking her way.

"Of course, I could mop it for you for just a little kiss." The boy moved in closer, pushing himself against Cristal and pressing her into the back cabinet.

"Stop," said Cristal in her strongest no-nonsense voice. "Get away from us."

The boy laughed and pressed in harder. But just as he got his face aligned with Cristal's, she heard the lady calling her name.

"Cristal, Fina, to the front now!"

Cristal and Fina ran to the front, ready to do anything to avoid the big boy, but not expecting the surprise of seeing Pastora Pati. Both girls hugged her tightly, not wanting to let go.

"Let's go, girls. Do you have anything here you need to get?"

"Nothing," they said in unison. And they left another horror behind.

"Thank you," Cristal whispered to no one in particular.

Chapter 33

A NEW HOME

CRISTAL and Fina thought they were going home. They were surprised when the car stopped in front of a different house. Had they been tricked?

"We can walk from here. I know where our house is," said Cristal quickly trying to open her door. "Thank you for the ride."

"No, Cristal. I'm sorry. I didn't explain when I picked you up. I thought you understood. You are gonna stay with us for a while, until your mamá can get things in better order to take care of you," the pastora said smiling hesitantly.

"Oh," she said, "we're fine. We know how to take care of ourselves. Thank you."

"That's not the deal, *mija*," said Pati. "We promised DIF that we would take care of you and Fina. That was the only way we were able to get you out. You both have to stay here for a while."

Cristal didn't know what to think. She had always fended for herself and Fina.

"Come on in, and let's eat some supper and talk about things," said the pastora. "Help me get the dishes out."

The two girls stepped suspiciously inside. They just stood and watched as the Pastora showed them their bed to share and where the bathroom was. It was inside! She pulled out some dishes and began to heat up the rice and beans and the few tamales left from her sales. She told them to sit, and the pastor came in with a big bottle of orange Fanta. They held hands around the table as the pastor prayed, "Father, thank you for bringing these girls back. We know they have a mamá and a house. Show us how we can help them have a loving home with a caring mamá. Thank you for this meal. Thank you for the brothers and sisters at church who are supporting us. Be with Toño, and show us how to help him too. And care for Ivan, wherever he is. Thank you for Jairo. Bless him for taking an interest in Ivan. Now help Cristal and Fina feel loved and welcomed in our home. Amen."

Pastor Pati served their plates, and the girls began to nibble self-consciously. Gradually their hunger took control, and they ate like the starving girls they were. Pastora Pati offered them each a slice of fresh watermelon, and they gladly accepted.

Suddenly Cristal hissed, "I don't want to help Toño. He is dangerous. Why did you pray for him?"

"We know he has done some bad things," said Pastor Miguel, "but we still want to help him if we can."

"No!" shouted Cristal, as she stood and ran out the door. She didn't know where she would go, but she wasn't going to be around Toño or any other mean boys again. She heard her name but kept running. She came around the corner of the store and saw Daniel and his little brother playing in front of his house.

"Cristal," Araceli called her. "Come here. Where's your sister?"

Cristal stopped running, lowered her head, and said, "She's with Pastora Pati."

"Do you want to come read with me?" asked Araceli. "I'm sorry I haven't been around to meet like I said, but Memo was in the hospital all week. We've had a crazy schedule. Come on over."

She sounded so nice. Why had Daniel been running away? The pastor had caught up to her, and she could see the pastora with Fina right behind. They were nice people too. Why had she been running away? The pastor called to her too, saying, "Cristal, Toño is not going to hurt you again."

Daniel ran up just then and said, "Toño's not going to be hurting anybody now. Policia Chuy took him away in handcuffs. It was so cool!"

"Daniel," said Araceli, "Handcuffs are not cool!"

"I know, Mamá, but it was so cool how just when Toño was about to smash my head in Chuy zoomed up on his motorcycle and handcuffed him just like in the movies."

"Are you OK, Daniel?" asked the pastora. "I heard that he punched you really hard." She looked to Araceli and her husband as she asked, worried that it might have been worse than he let on.

"He's fine," said his papá roughing his hair. "He needed to toughen up a little anyway. He might have to stand guard at our place at the *segundas* sometime while he earns back money to buy another scooter."

"I'm so glad he's okay," said Pati, "and Memo too."

"Thank you, Pastora. I told my husband about some of the changes at church and he is interested in helping with the soccer team."

"Come on girls, and let's see if we can beat these boys at soccer. Chuy says he's gonna have a strong girls' team."

The children ran to play, and Araceli talked some more to the pastors.

"So, how do you think it's going to go with the girls?" she asked.

"Well, they're not used to anyone caring about them. They have raised themselves. I'm not sure what to do about school yet either. I'm afraid that putting them in school right now would be a disaster. Fina would probably be fine at her age, but I don't want Cristal to have other kids making fun of her."

"I can help Cristal with her letters and reading. I had promised her before Memo got sick. Fina and Memo can play while Daniel works on his math facts."

"Thank you! Do you think I could drop them here in the morning when I go to my stand?"

"Of course! I can get to know them better while you get used to having little ones again."

"And now I need to get my tamales ready for in the morning. Is it OK if they play a little longer?"

"Pastora, yes! Thank you for all you have done, not just for these girls, but also for Daniel. I think he is appreciating his family a little more," she smiled.

The soccer game lasted until dark. Pastor Miguel joined in to help Daniel and Memo defend against their papá and the girls. Finally, Araceli called them in. "Come have some *limonada* before you go home."

Cristal and Fina ran to her. "Thank you," said Cristal. "Thank you," she said looking up to a God she was just beginning to know.

Chapter 34

ONE YEAR LATER

THE girls stayed with Miguel and Pati for the next year. They were able to enter school in the fall and just about catch up with their age groups by the end of the year thanks to help from Araceli and the other mamás. Chuy's mamá and Jairo took care of Ivan, giving him a room and bringing him over on Sundays to spend the day with his sisters.

Rubí needed more help than the little community could provide. She spent some time in a government drug rehab center to avoid jail time, but she couldn't stay clean for long. Pastora Pati found a Christian rehab ranch out from town. They were trying to persuade Rubí to give it a chance, but she hadn't reached rock-bottom yet. On good days Rubí visited with the girls who found it harder to show any affection for someone who had never shown them any. They remained respectful but distant.

Toño stayed at the *tribunal* for six months. Upon release, Toño stayed with his mamá, helping her repair their house. He rarely went out staying home to train dogs to become part of the K-9 police force. Pastor Miguel and Chuy visited him every week just as they had while he was incarcerated. His papá lost his job for driving a company rig under the influence and had not been seen in three months. But one blessing was his mamá began to attend the Iglesia Torre de Fe.

Daniel learned his math facts and became a top salesman at the *segundas*. He helped his papa every Saturday. Memo continued to have respiratory battles when the dirt clouds whirled through the neighborhood, but the difference was now the family could call on church family to help out. Life was still hard, but they were learning it was easier working together and helping each other out.

One Sunday morning as everyone was singing some of their favorite praise songs with Aurora's papá playing an acoustic guitar, Toño stepped into the little church and sat beside his mamá. Daniel, Memo, and Ivan sat together with Jairo and Chuy's family. Cristal and Fina sat with Aida and Aurora. Their mamas were in the *comedor* preparing for the children's activities and snacks. As the song ended, Pastora Pati welcomed everyone and gave Pastor Miguel the floor. He stepped to the front. There were no more microphones. He just talked to his flock.

"It has been a year since we started our new way of being a church. We have had some successes and some sadness, but overall, I believe that we have made a difference. I would like to make a change to our name. Our church is not about a building. It is about building people, building families. Instead of being a tower, I would like to change our name to *Familia de Fe*, a Family of Faith. Would someone like to help with painting the new sign? Thank you, youth! Also, as we have learned, there is always something to be done, someone who needs help, someone we can serve. Who can help with fixing Rubí's roof sometime this week?"

One by one the members offered to help with projects, and plans were made.

"Another announcement is that this afternoon we have a soccer challenge from the girls' team of the Colonia Sausal. Let's try to all be there to support our girls," Chuy said.

They read some from the book of Acts in the New Testament about the early church all working together as one and sharing everything. "Every day, they met together in the temple and ate in their homes. They shared food with gladness and simplicity. They praised God and demonstrated God's goodness to everyone. Acts 2:46." Sharing everything didn't always mean things. Sometimes it meant sharing time or sharing expertise like auto repair or reading skills. But each one had something to give, and each was called to give it.

After church as the girls were about to leave for their game, a van of gringos came by stopping at a vacant lot at the end of the street. They walked around observing the people as the translator told them about the neighborhood. She stopped when she saw Cristal and Fina dressed in their uniforms with their friends. "Do you want to tell them your story?" she asked. And so, they did.

Chapter 35

GLOSSARY

a BUELA-GRANDMOTHER
    abuelos- grandparents
    alabanza-praise
    buenas tardes-good afternoon
    capilla-chapel
    chanclas- flip-flops, sandals
    champurrado- thick, hot chocolate drink
    chicharrones-pork skins
    chicle-gum
    chile-any spicy pepper
    chorizo- a spicy Mexican pork sausage
    chucherías-junk food, snacks
    churros-fried crispy dough sticks
    colonia-a neighborhood
    colorado-red
    comal-flat iron skillet
    comedor- dining room, in this case used for serving hungry
children
    con salsa-with sauce
    Dolores-sorrows, pains
    familia de fe-family of faith
    frijoles-beans
    Gansitos-individual cakes such as Hostess

Gloria a Dios-Glory to God
gorda,gorditas-fat girls, chubby girls
gracias-thank you
gringo-anyone from the US
Hospital infantil-children's hospital
hijo-son
iglesia-church
mamá-mom
maquila-factory
mañana-tomorrow
mecánico-mechanic
mijo-my son (term of endearment)
milagros-miracles
papá-dad
prepa-high school
reggaetón-Latin rap music
Sabritas-potato chips and corn chips
Señora-Mrs. secundaria-junior high
segundas-flea market
sí-yes
sombra-shade
taller -a workshop
tarea-homework,chores
templo-church
tía-aunt
tiendita-convenience store
tortillas-flat corn or flour pancake like bread
tribunal-detention center
vecina-neighbor

Marion Surles has devoted her life to connecting two cultures. As a teacher of Spanish and English from pre-K to adult, Marion has tried to cultivate in her students a love and appreciation of both the American 'gringo' culture and the Hispanic culture. She believes we have so much to learn from each other, and we should value each of our contributions. During her school vacations, Marion spends her time in missions. Most recently in Mexico she formed a mission called Love and Literacy in a poor neighborhood of Ciudad Juarez. Love and Literacy encourages reading by providing activities and books in Spanish for all ages. Follow her adventures on her Facebook page Love and Literacy. Your purchase of this book will help this mission.

Made in the USA
Coppell, TX
21 March 2022